Story By
Scott Brown

Illustrations By
Daniel Fagin
David Chal
&
Brian Dobbins

Mr. Whap-o-pottamus is not your average guy

You can't even see him with an average eye.

But the Whap-o-pottamus is not that hard to find

All you have to do is keep an open mind.

Now Mr. Whap-o-pottamus has a friend or two

One is Frieda Fernfish who has a rose tattoo.

The other one is Larry who likes to hang around

He makes everybody laugh 'cuz he's a circus clown.

On Sunday they were talking and mostly on a whim

Decided they'd go to the shore and have a little swim.

The distance to the ocean was really kind of far

So Larry said he'd drive them in his circus car.

It took a half a day to make it to the beach

There they saw Shelly Sandshark swimming by the reef.

Now Shelly has a temper and a hammer head

So Frieda said that they should see the park instead.

Said Whap-o-pottamus, "If it were really hot..."

"...I would dive into the surf, but it's really not."

"And it would hurt my skin swimming in the salty foam,"

"So let's get some cotton candy and an ice cream cone."

Heading for the boardwalk the three were quite a sight

The humans who observed them discussed it through the night.

But if he even noticed he didn't seem to care

Mr. Whap-o-pottamus smelled taffy in the air.

While eating their candies and going to the car

They began to realize how lucky that they are.

Because they are true friends, they'll never be alone

It's been a big day, and now it's time to go home!

Mr. Whap-o-pottamus Goes to the Beach

Story By
Scott Brown

Illustrations By

Daniel Fagin

David Chal

&

Brian Dobbins

ISBN. 0-9763774-0-3

Brown & Fagin
Enterprises LLC.

Visit us on the web at
www.whapopottamus.com